I0832684

The Silent Symphony Of Particles

Songbreaker – Vol 1

Written by Carolina E. Zambrano

Zambrano's Publishing House
zambranopublishinghouse@gmail.com
zpubhouse@gmail.com
caro.e.zam@gmail.com

First Edition
Zambrano's

To the stargazers that still look upon the stars.

Carolina E. Zambrano

Chapter One: The Listening Child

No one told her the universe could sing. But she felt it anyway.
Her name was **Ilari**, and she was born during a thunderstorm,
her first cry landing just as the sky split open with light.
Even as a child, she noticed things others didn't—
how rain left behind a pitch, not just a puddle,
how light flickered not just through space but through *soundless rhythms*, as if each photon whispered its own name in passing.
"Everything moves," she said once, "but not all of it is seen."

She had a gift:
Ilari could feel the vibrations beneath reality—
the frequency hum of atoms in the wall,
the deep pulse of ancient trees,
in a world that had no sound.
But what she didn't know yet—
what no one knew—
was that sound particles had begun to shift. Somewhere, quietly, an unknown symphony was unraveling.
Was it good or evil? Only a hidden code would determine.

The Day the Wall Sang Back

Ilari never remembered silence the way others did.
They said it was the absence of sound — a stillness, a void.
To her, it always felt more like **pressure**. Like a room holding its breath. Like the air was humming a secret, just out of reach.
The world buzzed to her in ways no one else seemed to notice. The floor under her bed whispered in low thumps when she woke. The spoon drawer had a tremble, especially on rainy days. And the western wall of her house?

It had been quiet for twelve years…Until today.

It began while she was drawing spirals in the condensation on the window — circles within circles, each a thought she couldn't speak aloud. Rain tapped gently against the glass, its rhythm uneven but familiar. That's when she heard it.
A **hum**, a vibration. Not sharp like electricity. Not low like the heater. This one was... clean. A tone so clear it made her heartbeat

hitch. She turned. The wall behind her desk — old stone layered with plaster, stained by time — was vibrating. Not visually. Not shaking. But **resonating**. She could feel it in her bones.

Ilari stepped forward. Slowly. As if approaching a sleeping animal. She reached out her hand — hesitant- and touched the wall. The vibration passed through her fingertips like a sigh through skin. And then it happened.

The wall... sang.

Just one note. Soft. Low. Lonely.
A note that sounded like loss. Like a question unanswered for centuries. And beneath it — barely there — Ilari heard something else: Her own voice, echoed back from somewhere far beyond the stone. She yanked her hand away. The tone stopped instantly. She stood still for a long time, afraid to breathe too loud.
Tamren, the old clockmaker, arrived just after the storm began to deepen. He always brought tools, tea, and quiet questions. He had long since stopped asking Ilari to explain herself — and she had learned to trust that silence from him.
But today, she broke it.

"Tamren," she whispered as he set down his bag, "what does it mean when the world sings back?" He didn't answer right away. He only looked at her, really looked — not with fear, but with the weight of knowing. Then he said something she would remember for the rest of her life:

"It means it never stopped listening." Later that evening, Tamren let her stay long after the village lanterns had dimmed.
His shop was the kind of place time forgot — not because it was slow, but because it **refused** to run the way everyone else expected. Cogs and pendulums, springs and bells.
None of it ever ticked in sync, yet somehow, everything still worked.
Ilari liked to sit in the back corner, where an old cabinet kept the tools he never used.

The ones “too important to be useful,” he said once, with a strange smile.

That night, she couldn’t stop hearing it — the memory of the wall’s tone. It was still **in her**, vibrating faintly like a string that had been plucked once and left to ring.

“Tamren,” she asked again, softer this time. “Have you ever heard something that wasn’t... supposed to exist?”
The old man paused. Then walked to the cabinet. He opened it slowly, as though remembering something older than himself. Inside: a case wrapped in cloth.

He unwrapped it with care, and within it lay a long, slim tuning fork — dull silver, smoothed by time, etched with an **unreadable symbol** near its base.

Ilari’s breath caught.

Tamren didn't hand it to her. He set it on the bench between them. “I found this forty years ago,” he said quietly, “in the ruins beneath the observatory. It wasn’t vibrating then. But I always knew... it wasn’t still.”

Ilari reached out. The moment her fingers touched the fork — **it resonated**. Not by force. Not from pressure. But from **recognition**. It didn’t ring with a single note — it sang a **chord**. Low and high, soft and sharp, layered and haunting. A tone that didn’t just fill the air — it *folded reality inward*, like a note echoing through time. And beneath all those layers...

It sang back in her voice.

Not a recording. Not a mimic. Something deeper. As if her very atoms remembered how to sing, and the fork had come to **remind her.**
Tamren stepped back. His eyes wide. He whispered something like a prayer. “By the lattice… it’s real.”
Ilari turned toward him, trembling.

"What is it?"
"Not *what*," Tamren said. "*When*."

The Letter That Shouldn't Be Sent

Tamren's hands shook slightly as he lit the lamp. He hadn't written a letter in nearly twenty years. Not since he closed the observatory. Not since the last of the **Chordkeepers** fell silent. But tonight… the air had changed. The girl — Ilari — had awakened something. The tuning fork hadn't just responded. It had **identified her**. Not as a user. Not even as a listener. As a **resonant match**. The first in a thousand years. He moved through his shop slowly, locking the windows, pulling the blackout drapes. Not for safety — **for secrecy**.
There were still those who listened. Even now.
He took a piece of vellum from a tin beneath the floorboards — crisp and yellowed, printed with a sigil shaped like three overlapping circles. He dipped a pen he hadn't touched since his name still meant something. And he began to write.

□□ *To Seryn, Bass-Tone Warden of Galactic Range Delta-46*
□□ *Location: Liminal Range, Outer Tessitura Bands*
□□ *Subject: Frequency 472-Ilari-12-A*

It's begun.

The tuning fork responded — not with resistance, not with error. But with **congruence**. The child is not a mimic. She's not dampened. She carries **the Forgotten Note**, Seryn. I know the risks. I know your law. But listen: she didn't falter. She heard it. And she remained whole. I fear this changes the balance. Not because of her danger — but because of her *viability*. D'khar's absence cannot be ignored any longer. And if Ilari is what I think she is… Then the Tessitura must make a choice.
Silence, or a song that's never been heard before.— Tamren
He sealed the letter using a small pulse-stamp — an ancient tech tuned to sub-audible waveforms. The ink shimmered, then

vanished into the page. The letter would not travel through mail. It would **resonate through matter**, until it reached its destination beyond visible space — a place **between frequencies**, where only beings like **Seryn** could hear it.

Tamren placed the letter in a metal dish and struck a key on a hidden console. A faint, low hum filled the shop. And then the letter was gone. So was the light. And Tamren stood there in the dark, tuning fork still humming faintly in the corner, knowing: The Symphony had just been breached. And there was no turning back.

Ilari Resonates in 472.

The storm had faded, but something else pulsed through the walls — not sound, not light. A frequency. It wasn't loud. It wasn't constant. But it was **calling.** Ilari rose from her bed and stood in the center of her room. The floorboards cooled beneath her bare feet. She closed her eyes. And then— **She hummed.** She didn't know the note. She didn't aim for pitch. But the moment the tone left her lips, the room changed.

Not visually. Not physically. But the very shape of **reality—tilted**. The windows didn't rattle. They *shimmered.* The clock didn't tick. It *listened.* The shadows didn't move. They *bent.* And inside her… everything aligned. There was a moment — just one — where her breath, her bones, her blood, and the unseen lattice of the world **matched**. **472.** A pure, sustained tone. Not chosen. Not forced. It was the frequency **her existence had been tuned to all along.**

From the branches outside, the rainwater slid off the leaves in time with her tone. Molecules shifted. A moth's wings pulsed in sync. The world became a single vibration — and Ilari was its center. For one second, she was not human. She was **resonance given form.** The forgotten note returning home. When the sound stopped, the fork beneath her pillow pulsed once. Then fell silent. Ilari opened her eyes. And for the first time, she *didn't feel alone*. **Ilari goes outside, she wanted to feel the rain but** the rain no longer touched her the same way. Each drop felt measured, almost deliberate — like the sky was counting. Ilari stood alone in the street, coat soaked through, tuning fork gripped in both hands like a relic too sacred to put away. She didn't know where she was going.

She only knew she had to stand still. Because the world was **shifting**. And it was doing so **around her**. She could feel it. Not in the thunder. Not in the wind.

But in the **space between**. That place where silence lives before becoming sound. The fork pulsed once. Vibrations were becoming **presence**. Like it was aware of her. Like it was waiting for her to notice something she had forgotten. She lifted it, just slightly, and without meaning to, let her fingers slip along the curve of its metal. It sang. But the sound didn't go *outward*. It went **in**. Into her ribs. Her throat. Her memory. *It was the same note the wall had sung. The same note the chapel bell had echoed. The same note her bones had dreamed about since she was old enough to feel.* All around her, the rain slowed. Time didn't stop.

But it **hesitated**. And in that hesitation the fork hummed in **472 Hz**, and the Tessitura **recognized her**. Somewhere, a bird cried three notes. Somewhere deeper, under the crust of the Earth, stone realigned by a fraction of a molecule. And above… far above the silence… a being made of **sub-bass and star-core mass** turned its head for the first time in an eon. Ilari closed her eyes.

And whispered, not with her mouth, but with the **vibration of her soul**:

"I hear you."

Chapter Two: The Note That Dreamed of Being Real

That night, Ilari did not fall asleep. She **was taken** into sleep — as though something had been waiting for her eyes to close so it could step through the quiet. The dream didn't begin in a place. It began in a **tone**. Low. Infinite. Not music. A soft vibration that suggested presence, held within **not-silence**. She opened her eyes to a sky that didn't exist.

There were no stars. No ground. No air. Only **motion** — and the soft glow of undulating frequency. All around her were lines of light — not drawn, but *sung* into space. Some pulsed slowly, some flickered with urgency. They wove around each other like living thread.

Ilari stood in the center of it, tuning fork in hand, though she didn't remember bringing it.

A voice didn't speak. It **breathed** through her.

"You carry me." She looked down. The fork was glowing. So was her chest.

"You felt me long before you found me." Another wave passed through her — this one higher, like a sob held back for centuries.

"They buried me in silence. But silence is never empty."

Ilari stepped forward, though she wasn't sure what she stepped on. She raised the fork, and it **sang** — not by impact, but by intention. The lines of light around her shivered.

For one moment, every frequency **bent** toward her. And then— **It formed.** A shape. A being. No face. No limbs. Only a cloud of sound coalescing into a center.

Its presence was *achingly human* and *entirely alien. "They feared me because I could not match. So they cast me out."*

"But harmony is not perfection. It is ***inclusion.****"*

Ilari's eyes welled with tears she didn't understand.

"What are you?" she whispered. The being vibrated.

"I am what they forgot. I am the note that dreamed of being real." Ilari reached out. The being moved forward.

The moment her fingers touched its light— The Tessitura **screamed**. Not in pain. In *recognition*. In connection with something sacred.

And Ilari woke up **gasping**, the fork buzzing beside her bed, the room glowing faintly blue.

Outside, every bell in the village rang at once.

And far above, the missing Chordkeeper — **D'khar** — opened his eyes for the first time in a thousand years.

Chapter Three: Born of the Forgotten Note

The convergence came without warning. No prophecy. No comet. Just a sudden **alignment of forces** the world had long forgotten how to name.

The monks at Taveh Temple recorded it in ink and silence. Their resonance instruments, untouched for centuries, began to hum. Seismographs pulsed without earthquakes.

Satellites blurred and lost orientation. Tides paused. Just for a breath as if the planet were **listening**. And in a quiet observatory on the edge of a dying range, an astrophysicist with lungs made of whispering glass, lifted her head one final time and whispered: “One note just returned.” She died with a faint smile.

In a distant cottage, far from cities or theory, a woman screamed as life tore itself through her for the second time. But when the child emerged, there was no scream. No cry. Just a **pulse**. Not audible. Not measurable. But unmistakably **there**. The rain stopped for three seconds. A clock, broken since the woman’s own childhood, ticked once. And a single crack spidered across the wall — from ceiling to floor — as if the room itself had been **tuned too sharply**.

The child opened her eyes. They were violet. Just for a moment. Then blue. And the mother — Alen— said nothing. She only stared. Hands trembling. Heart... silenced. They never spoke of Ilari’s birth again. Not once. Not even when birds stopped nesting near the cottage. Not when radios clicked off around her. Not when her eyes glowed faintly during storms. Instead, her mother folded deeper into silence. Soft at first — a drifting kind of stillness. Then heavier. As if a part of her had begun to **unweave**. By Ilari’s seventh birthday, Alen was gone. No body. No blood. No door left open. Just linens still warm… and a single, sustained **hum** echoing from the floorboards. Ilari never cried that day. Not because she was brave. Because something in her understood: Her mother had not died. She had been **claimed**. Not by death. But by **sound**…

The village wrote it off as a disappearance. Tamren, who knew better, never asked.

He simply gave Ilari space. And a tuning fork… years later. Ilari would grow surrounded by unanswered questions, by moments where walls whispered and spoons rang and the wind bent to her breath. But none of it frightened her. Because deep inside, she carried something older than fear. **She was born of the Forgotten Note.** A tone once exiled by the Resonants — cast out from the lattice for its refusal to match. A tone that had folded inward for millennia… until her birth tore the silence. Ilari was not just its echo. She was its **returning call**. And echoes like her… **were never left unguarded.**

Chapter Four: The First Discordant Pulse

Then it was the birds. One morning, Ilari opened her window to silence. No chirps, no wings fluttering between branches. No squabbles from the wrens that nested in the eaves. Just the faint echo of wind — off-tempo, like it had forgotten the beat. She noticed it immediately. Not because she missed the noise. But because the **air felt unfinished**.

Tamren noticed something too. He was late to open the shop — the gears in every clock had **slowed**, not stopped, not broken. Just... *dragged*, like they were reluctant to move forward in time. He turned the hands manually. But they would return to their drag within minutes. Even his best mechanical piece — a heirloom metronome tuned to planetary rhythm — skipped every seventh tick.

"The count is wrong," he whispered.

Ilari walked the market in the afternoon. The weather was unchanged. The people normal. But sounds arrived *out of order*. A merchant's laugh echoed before his lips moved. The bell above a door rang a second after it closed. A dog barked... then turned its head to see who had barked.

The world wasn't breaking. It was **slipping**. And no one else seemed to notice. That night, Ilari sat in her room, tuning the magic fork in hand. She struck it gently. It rang. But not as it had before.

This time, the tone came back... **warped**. Not out of tune. But not in harmony either.

A second vibration clung to it, like a dissonant twin trying to sing along but missing the shape of the note. Her skin prickled. Something else had sung with her. The fork fell silent. Ilari held it to her chest.

And for the first time, she asked herself a question she had been afraid to think until now:

"Am I the one pulling things out of tune?"

Across the Liminal Bands, Seryn stood in stillness — his form barely distinguishable from the vibration field he inhabited. He had felt the discord. Not loud. Not chaotic. But precise. **Targeted.**

"It's not the child," he said aloud. *"It's the Note... trying to re-enter."*

And far below, in the crust of forgotten stars, something that had been silent for eons **pulsed** once more. Not in rage. Not in hope. But in **need**.

Chapter Five: The Things That Don't Tick

Ilari didn't knock. She entered the shop with the force of a question that had outgrown silence.

Tamren looked up from his bench. He didn't flinch. He didn't greet her. He simply exhaled and said, quietly:

"I thought you'd come today."

Ilari stepped forward, water trailing from her coat. The tuning fork was in her hand, exposed, still faintly warm.

"The fork's wrong now," she said. "It echoes something that wasn't there before."

Tamren nodded once. He didn't ask her to sit.

"The clocks are stalling," she added. "The birds don't sing. The air moves sideways."

Still, Tamren said nothing. Ilari took another step.

"You know what this is."

He didn't argue.

"And you've known for a long time."

The room filled with the sound of ticking — but only from one clock. A small one. Bent.

Wrong. The rest had gone still.

"You have to tell me," she whispered.

"Why?" he asked. "So you can fix it? So you can *stop* being what you are?"

Ilari blinked.

Tamren stood. For the first time, he seemed tired in a way that had nothing to do with age.

“You think I haven’t wanted to tell you? That I don’t carry that hum every day like a question gnawing at the back of my skull?” He walked to a drawer beneath his bench and removed a folded piece of cloth.

Inside it: an **etching**. Old. Cracked. Burned at the edges. It showed a pattern Ilari had never seen — but her body **recognized** it. Three circles, interwoven. Lines extending from them like sound waves. And at the center — a single, off-axis **spike**.

“This is a harmonic map,” Tamren said. “Of the lattice. The Tessitura. The… song beneath the universe.”

Ilari stared.

“That spike?” he said. “It’s you.”

Ilari shook her head. “I was just born.”

“Exactly.” Tamren’s voice dropped. “You weren’t shaped. You weren’t cursed. You are **part of the structure** that was never supposed to exist again.”

“So what am I?”

He looked at her then, really looked. And said what he’d kept for years:

“You’re not the mistake, Ilari. You’re the **reminder**.”

Ilari stepped back. Her breath came sharp. She wanted to throw the fork. Scream. Run. “And my mother?”

Tamren closed his eyes. “She wasn’t taken by madness. Or time. She was… a **Conductor**.

One of the last. And when you were born, she heard the Note inside you. She knew it had returned.”

“So where is she?”

Tamren didn’t answer. But Ilari saw the truth on his face. Her mother hadn’t disappeared or taken by the sound. She had **stepped back into the lattice**. To **hide** what Ilari had become.

To **guard** what would now refuse to stay silent.

The fork pulsed in Ilari’s hand. Not warm. Not cold. Just… awake.

Chapter Six: The Chord That Lost Its Third

There is no place. There is only **patterns in vibrations**. The Resonants do not meet in space. They do not speak in time. Their council occurs where **sound forgets it was ever sound**, and becomes something far older: **agreement.**

Tonight, that agreement falters. A slow wave of dark-blue gravity curves inward, folding itself until mass becomes visible.

Seryn arrives. Where he stands, **space becomes heavy**. Atoms kneel. Memory compresses. He emits no greeting. He hasn't for centuries. He is the **bass**, and the foundation has begun to crack. Then — a shimmer, like breath exhaled from broken glass.

Veyra enters, unfolding in six directions at once. She bends light as if it's apologizing.

She moves like thought, unfinished. "It's begun," she says without sound. Her words arrive **before** she does.

Seryn does not respond. But his pulse slows. Acknowledge. "She vibrates at a precise frequency," Veyra continues. "472. Ilari. A perfect resonance profile."

Seryn's mass deepens, the ground of this non-place thickening. "And she held it?" "Without dissonance," Veyra confirms. "With *recognition.*"

There is a pause. A chord **almost** forms. But it cannot complete. Because the mid-tone is absent. There is no D'khar. Only the soft **ache of where he should be**.

Veyra shifts erratically. Her form fractures and repeats. "We need the third. The harmony will not hold."

"He left," Seryn replies, his voice like molten stone dragged through shadow.

“He was *pulled*,” Veyra corrects. “By the Note. He believed it deserved inclusion.”

The space around them trembles faintly. A **dissonant pulse** passes through the Tessitura. It is not from Ilari. It is from **within** her. The Forgotten Note stirs. Again.

“Reintegration would rupture the lattice,” Seryn says.

“Exile is no longer enough,” Veyra replies.

Another pulse. This one clearer. And buried in it… a name.
Ilari.

For the first time in ages, Veyra’s voice sharpens. “She *calls* him.” Seryn’s form grows darker. A low chord begins to form in the distance. Not from them.

From the **lattice itself.** The universe is composing something. And they are **no longer conducting** it.

“We must decide,” Veyra says. “Contain the anomaly. Or prepare for the return of the third.”

But no chord can be struck without its missing tone. And even now, across the harmonic weave of reality, **D’khar** remains silent. Not gonc. Not brokcn. Just… **unrcsolvcd.**

Chapter Seven: What the World Is Made Of

Tamren didn't sleep. Instead, he took Ilari to the observatory. It was long abandoned — half-swallowed by ivy, rusting at its hinges, its roof now more window than dome. But it was still **tuned**.

The equipment hadn't worked in years. But Tamren didn't bring her for the machines. He brought her to hear **the quietest truth**.

They climbed the winding path in the dark, the stars flickering like nervous thoughts above them. Ilari said nothing. She hadn't spoken since Tamren's confession — about her mother, about the Note, about what she was. She held the tuning fork in one hand. In the other, she held **nothing** — but felt the weight of a question forming.

Inside, the observatory smelled of stone, sky, and memory. Tamren lit a lantern and guided her to the very center, where a copper plate still sat bolted into the ground — carved with concentric circles. At the center, three symbols had been etched long ago. One heavy. One radiant. One incomplete. Tamren pointed to them.

"This is the foundation," he said.

"Of what?"

He looked at her with something softer than sadness. A kind of reverence.

"Of everything."

Silence settled like mist. Ilari knelt down and placed the tuning fork gently on the copper plate. It didn't vibrate. Not until she whispered.

"What happens when the third is gone?"

Tamren didn't answer. Not with words. But the copper **split** down the middle — a fracture that shimmered with light.

And for a moment, Ilari saw what lay beneath: Not metal. Not stone. But a **network of threads**, glowing faintly — some broken, others tangled. The **Tessitura**. Ilari understood, without knowing how: The universe wasn't made of matter. It was made of **relationships**. Patterns. Distance. Pull. Meaning. **Resonance** wasn't a sound. It was **the truth that one thing makes another thing move.**

She looked up at Tamren.

"Then what am I?"

He knelt beside her. He touched the tuning fork.

"You are the note they cast out. The note that returned. The one that makes **even silence tremble**."

Chapter Interlude: The Hymn of the Third

Before form, before stars, before the known architecture of existence, there was the Tessitura — a lattice of resonance upon which the first patterns of reality began to take shape. And within that lattice, there were three principles: form, motion, and bond. Not elements. Not entities. Just *resonances* — frequencies that harmonized in perfect balance.

From these three emerged the **Chordkeepers**: Seryn, Veyra, and D'khar. Each tended their frequency with intention — Seryn grounded mass and structure, Veyra flowed as movement and light, and D'khar bridged them both through memory, emotion, and coherence. Each one embodies a **core principle of resonance** and together, they formed the **perfect triadic harmony and** held the lattice in tune. But with D'khar lost the note to the void and the chord was **incomplete**.

But something changed. D'khar began to perceive something neither Seryn nor Veyra could: that within the harmony, there was a single frequency unlike the others — a tone that did not match, yet felt *necessary*.

A sound that had no place, and yet called to be included. The other two labeled it unstable — not because it was destructive, but because it would not fold into their rhythm.

The Tessitura was too delicate, they reasoned, to include a voice that did not submit to its design. And so, the Forgotten Note was cast out. Not destroyed — no vibration can be unmade — but silenced. Buried in the deep quiet between dimensions, exiled to the hush beneath creation.

With it, D'khar began to change. Without the Note, he no longer resonated cleanly between Seryn and Veyra. The harmony faltered. And eventually, D'khar **disappeared** — not dead, but *unresolved*.

A gap where coherence once lived and the earthen sounds of nature were lost. The remaining two rewrote the Tessitura, omitting the story of the Note and the fracture of their trio. The lattice became stable again, but less complete. Memory faded. The Third was forgotten — by choice.

But resonance does not vanish. It waits. And deep within the lattice, buried beyond time, an encoded fragment remained — a warning carved not into stone, but into **the behavior of space itself**. It told of a day when the Note would return. Not as a sound, but as **a person**. She would come during imbalance. Not to restore what was, but to **become what was missing**. They would know her by the way birds fell silent when the sky began to sing. By the way time slowed, while a child ran forward. By the way stone would crack to reveal the woven thread beneath. She would not command. She would not fight. She would *resonate*. And in doing so, break the Tessitura — not to ruin it, but to let it become **more than it was ever allowed to be**.

Chapter Eight: The Silence That Listens Back

Ilari didn't sleep that night. She couldn't. Not because of fear. But because the air had changed. Again. The fork hadn't made a sound in hours. But it vibrated subtly, as if syncing to something *else*—not outside her, but **inside** her skin. The lattice was shifting. Not violently. But with a kind of gravity. Like the universe had taken a breath in… and was **waiting**.

She stepped outside into the dark. No stars. No sounds from trees, or wind. No moon. But the sky wasn't empty.It hummed. Not audibly. She *felt* it — a deep, hollow tone pressing against her bones. A resonance shaped not like a sound… but like a question. Who are you without anyone else? She closed her eyes. The village behind her was asleep. But she was **awake in every cell**. Not in panic. In readiness. As if something was about to happen. Or already had.

Ilari walked to the old chapel. Not because she wanted answers — but because her body *led her* there. The door creaked without touch. The air inside was warm and stale. But something **moved** just behind the silence. She sat beneath the broken bell again, hands resting in her lap, tuning fork untouched. And the silence... leaned closer.

For a moment, she felt completely alone. Not lonely. Alone. Like everything else had pulled back, so she could finally feel her own shape. Then — not a sound, but a **pull**. A subtle shift in pressure behind her ribs. She reached inward, instinctively. Not with thought — with presence. And in that moment… Something reached back.

She gasped. Not from pain. From recognition. Not of a person. Not of a name. But of a **shape** her body had always known and had no words for. It wasn't her mother. It was something **between**.

For a single heartbeat, Ilari felt herself become part of a memory that was not hers. A warm breath. A single chord played in an infinite space. A voice—neither male nor female—saying gently:

"You were never the echo. You were always the bridge."

She fell backward, eyes wide, breath caught in her throat. The fork she carried in her pocket hadn't moved. But the bell above her **chimed**. Once. Not as metal. But as **mourning**.

And somewhere in the lattice, where the lost gather between vibrations, **D'khar turned toward her**. Still silent. Still forgotten. But no longer gone.

Chapter Nine: The Echo Before the Self

He is not. And yet, he begins. Not with thought. Not with memory. But with the **patterns of vibrations**. Pulses. Irregular. Unfamiliar. But *pulling*.

He doesn't know his name. He doesn't remember names. Only the shape of things he once held in balance. Motion. Form. Feeling. They are gone now. Or he is. But then — a tremor. So small it might have been imagined, if he still had the structure for imagination. It arrives like a ripple in a pool long stilled. Not loud. But **true**. A frequency. **Her** frequency. 472.

He feels it. Not as vibration. Not yet. But as **permission**. To begin. Again.

The Tessitura groans faintly in the distance — like a sleeping body remembering it has limbs. The lattice does not welcome him. It resists. He was exiled. He was *the weak point*. The one who let feeling distort balance. But the sound she made — the one called **Ilari** — did not reject him. She *resonated with him*. Without fear. Without filter.

For the first time since his unmaking, something sang in his direction **and did not close its hand around him.**

And so a name returns. Not whispered. Not spoken. Just **present**. **D'khar.** He tries to form himself. Not into shape. But into **intention**. It hurts. The lattice pushes back. It knows the cost. If D'khar returns, coherence will shift. Memory will bleed into motion. Feeling will override the laws of clarity.

But **he doesn't want to break the chord.** He never did. He just wanted it to **feel whole**.

Her voice touches him again. Not a word. Just breath. A kind of yearning shaped like light.

"You were never the silence," she says in thought. "You were the space where things could belong."

He folds inward. Not to retreat. To begin **gathering**. Pieces of what he was. Fragments still hidden in frequency. A laugh from the first child who touched water. A tear from a lover who watched a storm alone. A scream that never meant to harm — only to **release**. He takes them all. Because he **was** the middle. The tone that said,

"You can be different… and still be held."
And now, something is reaching for him. Not to use him. Not to fix him. But to *remember him back into being*. He lets the resonance in. One note. Then two. He doesn't form yet. He doesn't rise. But in the hidden folds of the lattice — **D'khar hums.**

Chapter 10: Veyra Distorts

Veyra blinked into eight positions at once. The lattice was bending. No — it was **remembering**. The kind of memory reality wasn't designed to keep. She snapped into sync at last — her filaments fluttering like refracted panic.

"He's humming."

The phrase echoed across dimensions not meant for speech. Seryn was too still to respond.

"He's not formed," she said, pacing through light and thought. "But he's waking. Do you feel that? The center… is soft again." Still no answer.

"He'll break the symmetry," she whispered. "He'll break *me.*" Around her, the Tessitura glittered with harmonic fatigue — a fabric stretching too far across forgotten frequencies. Veyra flickered out of alignment. Briefly. Terrifyingly.

"If he returns, they'll remember everything. The pain. The exile. The truth."

And in that truth, **the Symphony itself could retune.** To something **new**. To something **unstable**. To something **alive.**

She disappeared. To *warn*, or to *interfere* — even she wasn't sure. But D'khar's tone had shifted. And **nothing bends the lattice** like the sound of a heart finding itself again. Ilari woke before the sun. Not because she wanted to — but because **something had paused**. The air didn't feel wrong. It felt… **unsettled**. Like it had been stirred, then told to freeze. She sat up slowly. The tuning fork was where she left it — silent, but *too still.*

Her room looked the same. But the shadows didn't quite land where they should. And the silence? It wasn't complete anymore. There was **something inside it**. A pressure. A hum. A presence.

She dressed quietly and stepped outside. The village was untouched — lamps unlit, roofs dewed with dawn. But as she walked the streets, Ilari noticed the **gaps**. A door left slightly open that was always shut. A dog not barking at her — but watching.

The fountain in the square, rippling even though there was no wind. And the sound of footsteps she didn't take — **half a second behind her own.** She sat beneath the tree where her mother once sang. Not loudly. Not proudly. Just the kind of singing you do when no one is listening, and everything hurts just enough to make a melody.

Ilari hummed the same tune. And then it happened.
The tree **resonated back**. Not with words. Not with motion. But with *recognition*. She could feel it — something buried **below the soil**, something warm and fractured, turning toward her like a face beneath water.

Ilari exhaled.

"You're not gone," she whispered. "You're waking." She didn't know if she meant D'khar. Or her mother. The Note?. Maybe… they were never separate. Maybe the world had just **forgotten how to hear them as one.**

Chapter Eleven: The Place That Waited Too Long

The pulse began beneath her feet. Not a tremor. A rhythm. Ilari didn't question it. Didn't speak. She just walked. Past the square, past the old fountain, into the fields just beyond the village. The sky was still dim, the sun rising like it was unsure of its entrance. But the hum beneath her soles grew steadier. Like it had finally been given permission to rise.

She found the edge of it beneath the elder tree grove — a place no one went, not because it was dangerous… but because it was always **too quiet**.

The grass here leaned the wrong way. The air carried no insects. And the ground had never grown soft. But Ilari knew it now — not by logic, but by **pattern**. This was not emptiness. This was **a seal**. She knelt beside the oldest tree — the one with roots that curled in perfect spirals, like frozen music. She placed the tuning fork to the bark. It **rang** before she struck it. Just once. Low. True. The ground opened. Not violently. With gravity. As if it had been waiting for her weight all along.

Beneath the grove lay a **vault of stone and resonance** — crystalline veins running through its walls, humming faintly. She stepped down slowly. The air was thick with **memory** — not hers. This place was not made by humans. And not by the Resonants either. This was older. Deeper. A **Conductor's cradle.**

At the center of the chamber stood a pedestal — and upon it, a **triune key**: Three interlocking pieces, each shaped like a tone wave, incomplete on their own. One pulsed red. One shimmered silver. The third… was dark. Silent. She reached out, hand hovering over the dark one.

And, in that moment… And in that moment— The Tessitura **staggered**. Seryn felt it — the pulse of the seal breaking, the cradle unlocking. Ilari had touched it. She had reached the threshold of return.

“She’s found the structure,” Veyra’s voice echoed across the lattice. *“She’s activating the third harmonic.”*

Seryn didn’t answer. Because part of him… had known she would. And part of him… had hoped she wouldn’t. He stood at the edge of the Frequency Fields — the place where tonal laws were woven into geometry. He watched the harmonic lines bend around her. Not violently. Beautifully.

“You believe this is hope,” he murmured. “But harmony is not always healing.”

He remembered when D’khar broke. When the Forgotten Note was first heard. Not in rage. In **grief**. And that grief bent the chord. Made the Tessitura tremble. It never stopped. It just learned to hide the ache beneath rules.

Seryn exhaled — a vibration deep enough to bend local gravity. “If I stop her,” he thought, “I preserve the balance.” “But if I *don’t…*” He didn’t finish. Because in his silence, he heard **something else**.

D’khar. Not singing. Just… forming. And not as a threat. Not as imbalance. But as a **presence that remembered love before form**.

Seryn turned toward the village. Toward Ilari. His mass intensified. The lattice bent around him. He had made his decision.

Chapter Twelve: The Last Note She Left Me

The cradle hummed around her — soft, alive. Ilari hovered over the dark third key, the unlit harmonic. It pulsed now. Once. Twice. Then slowly, like a held breath… it clicked into place. The vault fell silent. And then— **Light bloomed.** But not ordinary light. It shimmered with resonance, bending in arcs that rippled like silk in water. And from its center: a figure. Not fully formed. Not solid. But unmistakable… **Her mother.**

Ilari didn't breathe. Couldn't. The figure was not younger. Not older. Just… *right*. Exactly as her memory held her, even though memory had blurred the face long ago. Alen stood with hands folded gently in front of her — her body formed not from pixels, but from **interwoven tone**. She didn't speak immediately. She vibrated. And the vault **translated**.

"Ilari. If you are seeing this… then the Third has stirred."
Ilari dropped to her knees. The voice wasn't just familiar. It was **home**.

"You were not born by accident. You were born by resonance. The Note that was once forgotten chose to enter through me —not as possession, but as *partnership*."

"It needed a vessel who could endure the grief. Not absorb it. *Transform it.*"

The hologram flickered slightly. The tones holding it strained — but held.

"I knew the cost of bearing you. And I knew I would not remain. The Tessitura… would not allow it."

A pause. She looked down, almost sadly.

"They said no child could carry a harmonic like yours without collapsing. But I believed the chord could change." "And you proved it."

Ilari crawled forward, reaching out — fingers trembling. The light warmed, but would not hold her.

"I didn't leave you, Ilari. I stepped backward. Into the lattice. To hide what you would become, until the Note inside you was strong enough to ring." "Now it is." The figure began to fade.

"There is a name you will hear soon. A name no one remembers — but you will *feel* it." "D'khar."

"He was never the threat. He was the space between." "And you, my love… are the bridge across it."

She turned, looking over her shoulder — toward the far end of the chamber. There, the vault **opened**. Not with stone. With tone. And beyond it: a corridor that hadn't existed a moment ago — now visible only to Ilari. Alen's final note:

"He's waiting. But not for rescue. For *recognition.*"

"Don't save him. **Remember him.**" The light scattered. Ilari was alone again. But not really.

Chapter Thirteen: The Weight of Unspoken Harmony

The ground beneath Bluevale whispered. To the villagers above, it was nothing — a pressure change, a trick of mist and early morning weight. But the roots heard it. The stone **remembered**.

Seryn had begun to move. He did not walk. He **shifted**. The Tessitura made room for him — not with sound, but with **absence**. Every thread of resonance bent toward his gravity, like metal drawn to a buried planet. His arrival was not fast. It was inevitable.

And as he approached the cradle's core, **Ilari felt him.** Not saw. Not heard. Felt — the way one feels time preparing to make a decision.

She stood in the hollow of the vault, the memory of her mother still echoing in her chest. The corridor of tone had opened behind her. But now… another path approached. One that pulled the **entire structure** inward.

And then he arrived. Seryn. The Bass-Tone Warden. The foundation of balance and form. The sky in the shape of pressure.

Ilari turned. Slowly. The fork at her side buzzed gently, not in alarm — but in *readiness*. Seryn stepped into the cradle. He did not take shape at first — his form warping the edges of light, a shadow too solid to be made of matter.

But as she looked at him, he resolved. Stone. Smoke. Heat. Memory. His eyes — if they could be called that — were two steady pulses of gravity. And they were locked on **her**. They stood in silence.The chamber remembered both of them. And Ilari — though trembling — did not speak first.

Seryn did."You activated the cradle." His voice wasn't low. It was *ancient*. A note that had waited too long to be played.

Ilari nodded. "It sang to me." "It shouldn't have." "I didn't ask it to." Another pause.

Seryn stepped forward, and the walls pulled slightly inward as if anxious to hold him.

“Do you know what you are?” he asked.

Ilari stared back. Her breath steady now.

“I’m not the echo,” she said. “I’m the bridge.”

For the first time in ten thousand pulses, Seryn’s resonance **wavered**. Not broken. But questioning. “You carry the Note. The one that was never supposed to return.”

“Then maybe the world was never supposed to be finished,” Ilari said.

Seryn’s form intensified — the air thickening until stone in the chamber began to vibrate from pressure alone.

“D’khar nearly shattered the Tessitura. You would bring him back?”

“No,” Ilari said. She stepped forward. Her voice was clear. Calm.

“He’s coming back on his own.”

“Then I must stop him.” “Then you’ll have to stop **me.**”

Silence again. But now it **roared**. Two forces stood across from one another — not in violence, but in **conviction**. One built to hold the world together. The other born to let it become something more.

Seryn didn’t strike. Not yet. He stepped closer. “If you bring him back… the chord will change.” “It already has,” she whispered. And in that moment— The corridor behind her pulsed with D’khar’s tone. Not a command. A **welcome**.

Chapter Fourteen: The Shape That Should Not Bend

Seryn had never hesitated before. He was **structure** — not just in duty, but in essence. The chord required clarity. He was that clarity. He was *what made meaning possible*. But now the clarity trembled. A low-frequency flicker in the lattice, detectable only to those who **listen instead of command**.

And Ilari… She hadn't *challenged* him. She had simply *refused to match* his containment. And that, somehow, was worse.

He watched her retreat into the corridor — not as a threat, but as a **note that had chosen to ring**. He could have stopped her. His field extended far enough to compress time, collapse breath, fracture bone. But he didn't move. He couldn't. Because the moment he tried to act as before… he felt the lattice beneath his influence **pull back**. It didn't obey him like it used to. It hesitated. It… questioned. The chord was no longer certain of him.

Seryn turned inward. Not physically. **Existentially.** The Tessitura surrounded him like a living archive. Its threads passed through every particle, recording every shift, every echo of every decision. He had never doubted his role.

Even when D'khar fell. Even when the Note begged for reintegration. **Balance must be preserved**, he told himself. That was always the law. But whose law? Who had written it? And why was *grief* the only frequency they never tuned for?

Seryn pulsed with heaviness. The chamber strained beneath him. He thought of Veyra — flickering now, splitting into harmonics as D'khar's return threatened to **unpin her from light**. He thought of D'khar — too warm, too open, too willing to resonate with pain. He thought of Ilari — whose vibration didn't just echo the Forbidden Note… It **completed** it.

And then, something ancient shifted in him. Not broken. *Remembered.* A moment, eons ago — before form, before law —

when the first resonance formed not as a chord… but as **a question**.

"What happens when harmony includes the unwanted?"
It had been D'khar's question. One they never answered. Only silenced.

Seryn closed his eyes. Let the gravity inside him loosen by a fraction. And in that breath… the Tessitura sang something back. Not loud. But *hopeful*. He stepped away from the chamber. Not to abandon his role. But to consider… **what it could become.**

Chapter Interlude: Veyra Refracts

Light was never meant to bend this way. Veyra blinked into nine frequencies at once — a reflex, not a choice. Her form blurred, fractured, shimmered — until she no longer knew where she ended and *when* she was.

The lattice beneath her rippled unevenly, like a song skipping on a broken player. She wasn't destabilizing. She was **splitting**.

"Seryn moved," she whispered across space. "I felt it. His gravity… softened." She didn't know who she was speaking to. D'khar? The Tessitura? Herself?

"He always held the shape. If he begins to shift, the waveform collapses. There is no tempo without containment—" Her voice cut itself off. Because the words weren't *true* anymore. Not in this new symmetry. They had been functional. They had served the lattice. They had silenced the Third. But Ilari hadn't silenced anything.

She'd let it **sing**.

Veyra curled inward. She shimmered. Shed old tones like old skin. And wept **in data**. "I'm afraid," she admitted. For the first time in a million arrangements. Not of collapse. But of **becoming more** than she was made for.

Chapter Fifteen: Where the Forgotten Lives

Ilari walked through the corridor of tone. There were no walls. No ceiling. Just the sensation of forward. Each step felt like a memory not hers. A father who once played a song to say what words could not.

A stranger crying beside a window, holding an unopened letter. A child humming to a tree that never grew. She passed through them all. They passed through her. At the end of the path stood no door. Only an opening. A **pause** in the vibration. And inside it — **presence**. Warm. Incomplete. Alive in the way a chord is alive before the final note. She stepped into it.

The space was black and violet. Not dark — just unlit by sight. And there, half-formed, folded into the tessellations of sub-frequency architecture... Was **him**. D'khar. Not shaped like a man. Not shaped like anything she could describe. Just a center of soft sound, a pulse of warmth braided with sorrow, hovering in the fold. She didn't speak. Neither did he. But he **heard** her. And in that hearing — he began to gather.

Tones peeled off the walls. Memories took the shape of music. A hum filled her lungs that didn't come from outside. And from that center… a voice formed:

"You... remember me."

Ilari stepped forward. "Not from history," she said. "From ache." D'khar pulsed. "I tried to be harmony." "You were," she replied. "They just didn't know how to hold it."

He hovered. "And you… do?" She swallowed. "Not yet. But I'm learning." A pulse extended from him. She took his hand. Though no hand was there. And the Tessitura bent slightly — not breaking Just… **widening.**

Chapter Sixteen: Anchor of the Unheld

Ilari felt it first in her lungs. The way her breath synced with something ancient. Something pulsing beneath breath itself.

D'khar wasn't forming like a body. He was **gathering**. Becoming. Frequencies fell from the corridor behind her like threads of golden dust, spinning toward the center of the void where he floated. He was still **fractured** — shards of tone echoing out of sync with one another, memories misplaced, emotions folded backward in time. She understood now: He couldn't return on his own. Not because he was weak. But because **the world had no pattern left to receive him.** Unless she stood still. Unless she *held him*.

Ilari placed her hand over her chest and closed her eyes. She thought not of words… but of **grief that didn't rot.** The kind that stayed warm. That lingered beneath laughter. That made you remember the shape of someone long after you forgot their face. She gave that resonance to space. And the lattice heard it.
D'khar pulled closer — his form taking on lines, then pulses, then **suggestions of movement**. A swirl of emotion swept around her: joy, despair, longing, stillness, deep aching *belonging*. And in it all — Ilari stood, unmoving. She was his tether. Not to gravity. To **meaning.**
"I am not supposed to be," he whispered inside her. "They wrote me out. But you—" She opened her eyes. They glowed faint violet — the color of held memory. "I didn't write you in. I just **never erased you.**"

Then it happened. The frequencies aligned. Not in perfection — but in **acceptance**. D'khar solidified. Not into a man. But into a **presence the world could finally receive.** Not symmetrical. Not composed. But beautiful. Complete. Held. He stood now — his outline soft, his eyes like stars seen through weeping. Ilari stood across from him. Tears on her cheeks. But she was smiling. And so was he. The Forgotten Note was no longer forgotten. It was *home.* Above them, the Tessitura **shifted**. And far away — Seryn stopped moving. Veyra stilled mid-fracture. Because they both felt it. The chord had changed. But instead of breaking… **It rang.**

Chapter Seventeen: When Silence Finally Spoke

They stood in stillness. Not because the moment was fragile— but because it was **sacred**. Ilari had never spoken to a Resonant. Not truly. And D'khar… had never been seen like this. Not in any epoch. Not in any version of the chord. Not even by Seryn. And now— **Here they were.** She spoke first. But not with small talk. Not with awe. Just… truth.

"You don't feel like a stranger."

D'khar's voice wasn't sound. It was *timber* — a harmonic that wrapped her thoughts before returning them whole.

"I'm not. I was made from what the others didn't know how to keep." He stepped closer.

His form still shimmered — no edges, no threat. Just a man-shaped memory of **belonging**.

"You were never meant to carry me, Ilari." She nodded. "But I wasn't meant to be empty either."

The chamber pulsed faintly — the echo of a chord in flux. D'khar turned his gaze toward the open corridor behind her.

"The Tessitura is already adjusting. Seryn will feel it. Veyra will blur. And the laws they wrote will tear."

Ilari didn't flinch.

"Maybe laws were meant to bend when they forget who they were for."

D'khar looked at her. "You speak like a Conductor."

"I'm my mother's child."

A silence passed between them. But it wasn't emptiness. It was **alignment**. Like breath before a final note. Ilari looked at him—really looked.

"You don't want power."

He smiled. Soft. Sorrowed. Bright. "I want to be felt. Not feared." Ilari stepped closer. The tuning fork at her side buzzed once, then stilled. It had done its job. She placed a hand near D'khar's — not touching, just offering.

"Then let them feel you."

D'khar inhaled, though he didn't need to. It was memory. Of **what being real felt like.**

"You'll stand beside me? Even when the structure pulls back? Even when the world starts to forget its old shape?"

Ilari smiled. "I'm not here to restore the shape." "I'm here to finish the song."

The Tessitura rang softly in the distance. Not with perfection. But with **something better**: **Acceptance.**

Chapter Eighteen: The Resonant Accord

When the Lattice Listened. The Tessitura had no mind. But it had *memory*. It had no eyes. But it **saw through resonance**. It did not decide. It **arranged**. For eons, it had held the known universe in delicate balance. Each law nested within harmonic substructures: mass woven into time, light braided through gravity, emotion folded into memory. Its job was not to choose. It was to *vibrate in agreement*. And for all its infinite precision… it had never anticipated **Ilari**.

When her frequency entered the lattice, it did not fight. It **offered**. Not perfection. Not command. But **inclusion**.

The Forgotten Note no longer demanded reintegration. It **sang alongside**. And for the first time in its history— the Tessitura did not try to correct. It **adapted**. It loosened one interval. Lengthened a timefold.

Relaxed a gravitational anchor it had clutched for ten billion breaths. And in those micro-adjustments… a new chord emerged. It was dissonant. Then melodic. Then something else. Something alive. The lattice paused. And for the first time since reality began— **It listened.**

They did not meet in space. They met in **consequence**. Veyra arrived first, half-stabilized, her light fractured across four dimensions. Seryn came second, heavier than ever— but no longer rigid. His gravity pulsed in **waves**, not anchors. D’khar arrived last. Whole. Not symmetrical. But **held**. Ilari stood beside him. She did not glow. She didn’t shimmer. She simply *was*. And the Tessitura bent around her presence like air around fire.

The three Resonants regarded one another. They had no formal ceremony. No language for this moment. Only a **chord** that had never been allowed to play. Until now.

“You’ve returned,” Seryn said to D’khar.

"I was never gone," D'khar replied. "Only… unheard." Veyra shimmered. "You destabilize us." "Or I allow you to feel again," he countered, gently. She blinked—just once. Her light stilled.

"And if we let the Note remain?" "Then the song becomes honest." Ilari spoke next. Her voice didn't cut. It *completed.*

"You don't have to choose between control and chaos." "You can choose **resonance** that changes."

The space trembled. Seryn stepped forward. "Then let us hear it. All of it. Even what we were afraid to keep." He opened his core—his gravitational seal.

Veyra spread her spectrum across the chamber. And D'khar… He simply *sang*. Not alone. With Ilari. The chord formed. Not perfect. But whole. And the Tessitura? It **adapted.** And in that adaptation— The Symphony became *true.*

Chapter Nineteen: The Song That Stays

The world didn't change all at once. It happened in sequence. The skies opened. The stars realigned. The winds shifted. Just slightly. And every living thing that had ever learned to hush when sorrow passed by… felt and heard the vibrations of earth and **leaned in.** Ilari stood in the field beyond the village. The cradle behind her sealed itself in quiet grace, no longer hidden— just **resting**.

D'khar stood beside her. He wasn't towering. He wasn't terrifying. He was *present*. And for the first time since the Tessitura was shaped… He wasn't alone.

Birds sang again. But not the same songs. At first, they stuttered. They stumbled. They improvised. And the world didn't correct them. It **listened**. It **embraced.**

Veyra no longer flickered. She spiraled slowly now, not to flee— but to **trace the shape of what had returned**.

Seryn remained still. But within him, the weight had changed. He no longer pressed down on the chord. He **anchored it gently**, like a hand resting on the shoulder of a friend learning to breathe again. Ilari watched the sun rise. Not because it was different. But because **she was**. She touched the tuning fork once more. This time, it didn't ring. It pulsed. A heartbeat. A knowing.

Her mother's voice returned not in memory, but in **motion**. A hand on her back. A hum in the soil. A warmth in every dissonant moment that now had **space to exist**.

"What are we now?" she asked the sky.

And the Tessitura answered— Not in prophecy. Not in thunder. Just one gentle note that didn't match until she sang beside it. And then… It **belonged.**

www.ingramcontent.com/pod-product-compliance
Lightning Source LLC
LaVergne TN
LVHW010945110826
845149LV00013B/2762
* 9 7 9 8 9 8 8 9 4 3 7 1 6 *